THE DIVIDE

Michael Bedard ✖ Illustrated by Emily Arnold McCully

A Doubleday Book for Young Readers

A Doubleday Book for Young Readers
Published by
Bantam Doubleday Dell Publishing Group, Inc.
1540 Broadway
New York, New York 10036
Doubleday and the portrayal of an anchor with a dolphin are trademarks of Bantam Doubleday Dell
Publishing Group, Inc.

Library of Congress Cataloging-in-Publication Data
Bedard, Michael.
        The divide / by Michael Bedard ; pictures by Emily Arnold McCully.
            p. cm.
        Summary: Unhappy when her family first moves out to the plains of Nebraska, the young Willa
Cather comes to appreciate the beauty of her new home.
        ISBN 0-385-32124-4 (alk. paper)
        1. Cather, Willa, 1873–1947—Childhood and youth—Juvenile literature.   2. Novelists,
American—20th century—Biography—Juvenile literature.   [1. Cather, Willa, 1873–1947—Childhood
and youth. 2. Authors, American. 3. Women—Biography.]   I. McCully, Emily Arnold, ill.   II. Title.
PS3505.A87Z57   1997
813'.54—dc20   96-14726
[B]   CIP
                                                                             AC

Manufactured in the United States of America
The text of this book is set in 16-point Windsor Light.
Book design by Trish Parcell Watts
October 1997
10 9 8 7 6 5 4 3 2 1

for Martha
—M.B.

to Harriet Shorr
—E.A.M.

Willa stood at her window, looking one last time at the grass sloping down to the willowed stream, the road winding off into the wooded hills, the meadow marbled with sheep. Gone, forever gone.

The house stood all but empty—bare and still. She gathered up a few last precious things. Her footsteps echoed on the stairs. They seemed to say she was a stranger there. She felt an ache inside that made it hard to breathe.

Outside, the wagon waited, loaded with what little they could bring. The rest had been sold away. Mama sat by Papa, the baby at her breast.

Beside them sat Grandma, bundled in her shawl. In the back the two boys were squeezed among trunks and boxes.

"Come on, Willie," they called, and she climbed in with them.

As the wagon rumbled down the road, Old Vic, their dog, trailed along behind. She wore little leather pads to protect her feet.

On the way to the station they stopped. A neighbor farmer took Old Vic and chained her up. The sound of her barking followed them a long way down the road.

The train stood restless at the station while they loaded their things
and scrambled on. They had never been on a train, and the boys' eyes
were wide with wonder.

But Willa sat by the window, still as stone, and watched her world
slide away. The mountains raced in vain against the blue stone sky.
She clutched her trunk on her lap as if it were her life. As they sped
off down the track she spied Old Vic, broken free, chasing after them
across the fading fields.

They were bound for the Divide, a place on the prairies, many miles away. A land full of promise, Father said. They would make a new life there.

Day followed endless day. They rode in coaches all the way, sleeping in snatches, curled up on the seats, the red plush stinging their cheeks. The baby squalled, the children fussed. The country flew past like the smoke from the engine, dissolving into distance.

The coach ahead was the immigrant car: families huddled with their boxes and bundles, too few clothes against the cold. Strangers, like her, in a strange land.

One day, toward evening, they crossed a broad river, and Father said
they would soon be there.

Through the window of the train Willa looked out on a flat, empty
land, as bare as a strip of sheet iron. A country not a country, but a sea
of rusty grass.

How quietly the train ran now, as if the wheels whispered, steel to steel.
All night long they traveled, deeper and deeper into the iron land. There
were no lights, no towns, only the weight of darkness pressing down.

At last she fell asleep. She dreamt she was running through the woods back home with Old Vic.

Father woke her to say they had arrived. She scrambled half asleep into the early light. They stood with their baggage on the wooden platform and watched the train ride off toward the sky.

A wagon waited. Quietly they loaded their things and began the long ride onto the Divide.

It was early still. The boys slept, bedded on straw, beneath a buffalo skin. But the jolting of the wagon kept Willa awake. She hung on to the edge of the wagon box and peered over the side.

The road was just a faint track through the swaying grass. There were no farms, no hills, no trees, only the flat, silent land beneath the vast, unbroken sky. She felt they had come to the end of things.

Father had said one must be strong in a new country, and she swore to herself she would not cry. But now and again as they drove on into day there would be a stirring in the grass, and a lark would fly free on sudden wings, break the silence with its song, then drop to the grass again. Each time, she felt sure her heart would break.

The house rose from the sea of grass to meet them. It was a tall, gaunt thing of weather-beaten boards, huddled in a hollow from the wind. Behind it stood a barn, a field, a few sad trees.

They settled in by degrees. The bedrooms lay aboveground, the kitchen below, hewn into the soil. They ate from tins. A week crept by.

Willa sat on the bed, her treasures laid out on a quilt. A music box, a scrapbook made of cloth, a few books, seashells—memories. She would not put them out; she could not, would not stay. No one could live in such a place.

The land was a wild thing, strong and stern and still. She felt it did not want them there. It wanted to be left alone.

But then spring came, like a shy child bringing gifts of flowers to the door. They hid in the low places on the land. Ironweed, shoestring, snow-on-the-mountain. Buffalo peas, blooming pink and purple by the road.

It was not the spring of home, but a new thing. Spring itself. A high, restless wind that teased the curtains like a playful pup. Warm, pale sunshine; clouds drifting in a china sky. The silent land stirred into life.

In the daytime Father worked the fields. The strong, rich smell of fresh-plowed soil filled the air. Small green fingers stretched toward the sun.

Grandma laid a garden near the house. Willa helped her plant the seeds. They carried a hickory cane with a steel tip as they walked the path. Rattlesnakes sometimes slithered from the grass.

One night Willa took her books out of her trunk. She read aloud while Grandma pieced the patches of a quilt.

Summer came, long and hot. Father made her a present of a pony, and Willa roamed free over the open fields of the Divide.

The road was lined with sunflowers now. Father said they sprang from seeds the first settlers had dropped from their wagons as they crossed this land, to mark the way for those who followed.

She followed it now and found a pond where ducks came, a solitary elm that grew from a deep cleft in the ground. It had fought so hard to grow; she would visit it as if it were a friend. She sat within its shade and played her music box and watched a hawk turn circles in the blazing sky. In this flat land these were precious things.

Neighbors were few, scattered like the wildflowers in the low places on the land. Swedes and Danes, Bohemians and Norwegians. They had little, their houses built of sod cut from the ground, nothing but the land itself in another shape.

The old women understood her homesickness, and quickly they became friends. She brought their mail from the post office, ran errands to the neighboring farms, watched them at their baking or butter making. They told her stories of the Old World across the sea.

They had little English. Their speech was slow, their words were spare. She felt that each word counted as twenty; so much was left unsaid.

At home she took the shells out of her trunk and turned them in her hand. They were so plain without, so pearled within.

Autumn was the season of splendor: the miles of copper-colored grass drenched in brilliant sunlight, the sky as bright as blue enamel.

As she rode home down the sunflower-bordered road, she thought of that first long ride onto the Divide. It had seemed to her then that they had come to the end of things. But it was only a beginning again.

As she looked out over the sunlit land, she knew the love the farm women felt for it. It seemed beautiful to her now, strong and still and free.

The scattered fields of wheat and corn: dark and light, light and dark. Treasures laid out on a quilt. Precious things.

In the long grass she could hear the crickets sing. She felt that
her heart hid down there too, with its own song waiting to be sung.
Over the field there was a sudden rush of wings. A lark flew from
the long grass up into the sun. The silence rang with its rapturous song.

AFTERWORD

Willa Cather was nine when her family moved to the farm on the Divide in 1883. They remained there for almost two years, then moved to the nearby town of Red Cloud, Nebraska, sixteen miles to the south. Here Willa passed her teenage years. The family lived in a rambling white frame house. The children slept in the attic, a magical place with a peaked roof, rafters, and low, sloping walls. Willa slept at one end in a little room divided from the rest. Weather sifted through the cracks; moonlight silvered the floor. She hung rose-patterned paper on the walls; it is there still.

As a young woman Willa moved east and worked for many years as a journalist and an editor of magazines. But she often returned to Red Cloud, and she never forgot those first months on the Divide. She often said it was the most important time in her life.

It is as a writer that people remember Willa Cather now. In the novels that won her fame, she wrote of those first settlers on the Divide, of the harsh beauty of that flat land, and of the women who had taught her what strength and courage meant. Her heart hid somewhere in the long grass always. It sang a new song that had never been sung before.